A MESSAGE TO PARENTS

It is of vital importance for parents to read good books to young children in order to aid the child's psychological and intellectual development. At the same time as stimulating the child's imagination and awareness of his environment, it creates a positive relationship between parent and child. The child will gradually increase his basic vocabulary and will soon be able to read books alone.

Brown Watson has published this series of books with these aims in mind. By collecting this inexpensive library, parent and child are provided with hours of pleasurable and profitable reading.

Willow
The Witch's Cat

Text by Maureen Spurgeon

Brown Watson
ENGLAND

What's your idea of a witch's cat?

A cat like me, perhaps – black, with sharp, pointed ears, big eyes and a long tail?

And the witch? Well, you probably wouldn't expect her to be forgetful and stupid, getting into all sorts of muddles and screaming "Willow!" at the sight of a mouse – would you?

But then, you probably don't know my mistress, Wumpet the Witch! I heard her say once that she got her name from a spell which had gone wrong.... And, with Wumpet around, that's nothing unusual!

"Wee-willow-wickety... er--er--Wicky-won-wackety..." (Wumpet has never quite managed to remember the right words for a spell, yet!) "Or, is it Winny-wack-williby----?" No wonder her magic gets all mixed up!

I can usually see when spells are starting to go wrong, long before Wumpet does. That's how it is that I always manage to get out of the way in time, and she doesn't!

But, whether I hide under the stairs, or up in the attic, Wumpet is never far away! So you can guess how pleased I was to find a hole in the fence, just big enough for me to squeeze through.

"Hello," said a voice, not a bit like Wumpet's. "You're the cat from next door, aren't you?"

Without thinking, I mewed at her, "Yes, that's right," hoping she would understand me. And, she did!

What's more, she seemed to
know about Wumpet, too.

"I've seen you with that silly old
witch," she said and stroked my
head. "Would you like one of my
cheese crackers?"

Cheese crackers! I had never tasted cheese crackers in my whole life! Then she brought me a saucer of rich, creamy milk and an old blanket, in case I wanted to lie down.

"Don't forget that isn't our cat. He really belongs to someone else," came another voice.

Jenny laughed. "He is just like a friend come round to play, Mummy. That's all right, isn't it?"

And, so it was. Jenny never once said a word about Wumpet, or about me being a witch's cat. That was just one of our secrets.

If Wumpet only knew how we laughed at her.

And what with all the snacks Jenny kept feeding me, I was getting fatter and fatter – which meant the hole in the fence got bigger and bigger, until even Wumpet could see it!

Of course, I squeezed back through the hole as quickly as I could, but it was too late!

"So!" she screeched in her loud, witchy sort of voice. "This is where you go when my back is turned, eh?"

She stamped back indoors, and came out waving a rolling-pin!

"My magic wand!" she said with a wild cackle. "Now I can get one of my spells working on this."

Jenny and I held our breath.

She straightened her pointed hat and began.

"Minny-mon-moony, er–ahem! ahem! Cold ginger beer!

Er—great big hole, please disappear!"

Poor old Wumpet! She didn't realise she had holes in her skirt and her magic made the holes disappear, until there was no skirt left!

But the hole in the fence was still as big as it ever had been....

Next day, we watched Wumpet dragging out her cauldron.

"Magic potion!" she kept puffing to herself. "That's what I need!" She gave a snort in our direction, but we pretended not to notice.

"Dandelion and daisy root! Lollipop sticks and football boot! Hair of maggot, slice of rain! Put my fence to rights, again!"

It seemed that this time, Wumpet had actually got the words right for once!

And can you guess what happened next? Nothing at all!

All day long and half the night Wumpet kept on with that spell, getting angrier and angrier and the words more muddled up each time.

"Wonder what she's going to do next?" said Jenny. She was trying hard not to laugh out loud, but it wasn't easy – not when we could see Wumpet getting tangled up in armfuls of long twigs and more spell-books!

Wumpet took a long twig and drew a circle in the soil.

"Circle and square, drawn here today, please make the hole in my fence go away!"

"Drat!" she shouted. "Drat, drat!"

"Is that part of the spell?" giggled Jenny.

"Drat!" Wumpet screamed again. "I forgot to dip the stick in the juice of a red jelly-bean! I'll have to go and fetch one!"

By now, Jenny was laughing so much that her Daddy came out to see what was happening.

"Er, it's the cat from next door," said Jenny hastily. "He looks so funny, squeezing through the fence."

"Yes, Mummy did mention it. I'll fetch my tools, Jenny, then we can patch it up with a bit of wood."

"Don't suppose the old lady next door has noticed it," he remarked, as he sawed and hammered.

When Wumpet came out again and saw that the fence had been mended, she gave a whoop of delight.

"My magic worked, after all!" she cackled. "One of my best spells! Kippers for tea tonight, Willow!"